THE CAT OF THE CORCORAN

THE CORCORAN GALLERY OF ART

WRITTEN BY
ANN ZANE FELS

ILLUSTRATED BY
JOHANNA CRANE

For art lovers of all ages and the hard-working docents of the Corcoran Gallery of Art

Special thanks to Jeanette Ortiz-Osorio and Sarah Zane Schramm

· · · · • • • ● ● ● ● ● • • · · ·

Copyright © 2015 by Ann Zane Fels. 698932
Library of Congress Control Number: 2015912569

ISBN: Softcover   978-1-5035-9207-0
        Hardcover   978-1-5035-9206-3
        EBook   978-1-5035-9208-7

Print information available on the last page

Rev. date: 02/18/2016

To order additional copies of this book, contact:
Xlibris
1-888-795-4274
www.Xlibris.com
Orders@Xlibris.com

INTRODUCTION

The Corcoran Gallery of Art, where our tale takes place, was the first art gallery in Washington, D.C. All of the works of art written about in this book are in the Corcoran. It was founded by William Wilson Corcoran in 1869. He was a founding partner of Riggs Bank and collected American art.

Senator William Andrews Clark was a very wealthy man who had made a fortune mining copper in Montana and became a senator from that state. He loved France, Europe and art. He had an extensive collection of European art objects, including paintings, rugs, the "Salon Doré" and more. The collection was donated to the Corcoran after his death in 1925.

In late 2014, the Corcoran Gallery of Art became part of the National Gallery of Art in Washington, D.C., and the Corcoran College of Art and Design became part of the GW Columbian College of Arts and Sciences.

A cat named Midnight lived in the basement of The Corcoran Gallery of Art. He slept in the daytime because his job was to catch mice at night.

He loved being in the quiet gallery at night. The only person there was his friend Joe the security guard.

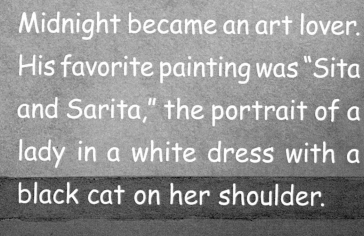

Midnight became an art lover. His favorite painting was "Sita and Sarita," the portrait of a lady in a white dress with a black cat on her shoulder.

He stared at her for so long that he fell asleep and dreamed that Sita climbed down and out of the painting!

As he looked into her beautiful eyes, he fell in love with her.

Together, Midnight and Sita ran merrily and chased François, the French mouse, into the "Salon Doré"-- the golden room full of French treasures!

They chased him up onto the mantel and over
Queen Marie Antoinette's clock.

François was too fast
and escaped behind
the wall. He peered
out at them through
his mouse hole.

Midnight and Sita gave up trying to catch François and scampered off to see "Mount Corcoran"--the grand landscape painting.

This time, they jumped into the painting, but a big black bear chased them. They quickly climbed up a tree to get away from him.

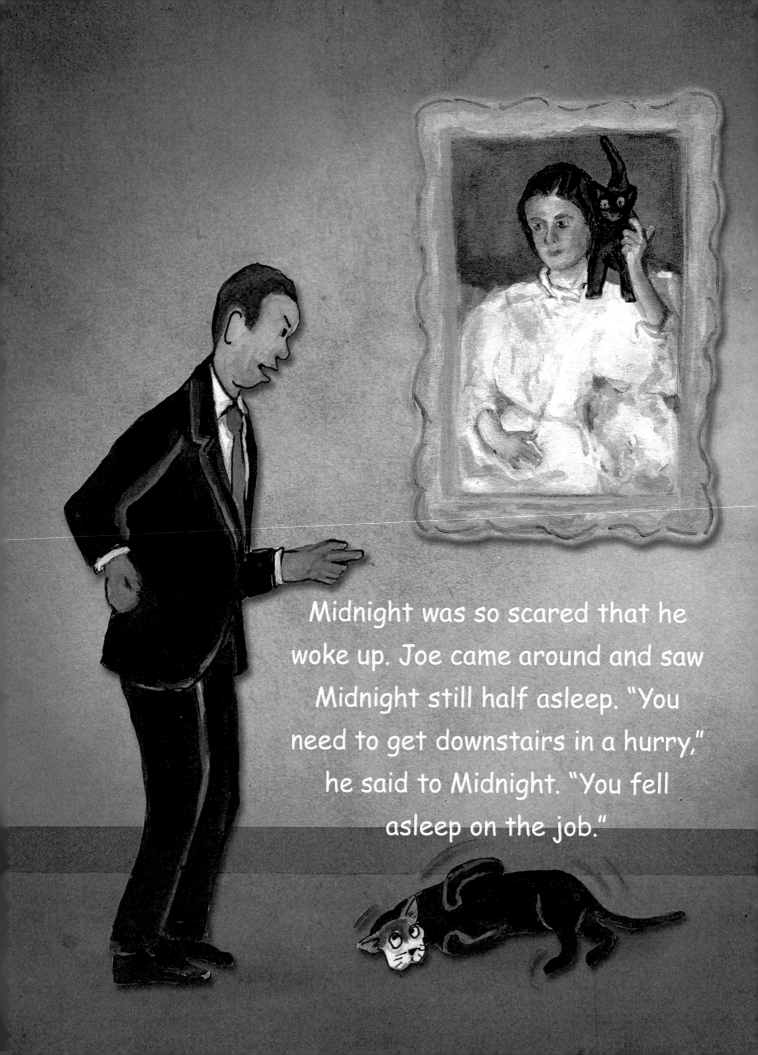

Midnight was so scared that he woke up. Joe came around and saw Midnight still half asleep. "You need to get downstairs in a hurry," he said to Midnight. "You fell asleep on the job."

Midnight raced off so fast that he bumped into the sculpture of "The Mountain Man." "Whew-- how scary--for a moment, I thought that it was a real horse!"

Running quickly down the stairs, he was so happy to return safely to his cozy basket.

"That was such fun," he thought.
"Maybe tomorrow night Sita and I can visit Niagara Falls."

THE END

Although this is THE END of the story, Midnight will continue his adventures with art, and hopes that you will, too!

ABOUT the Artists, Paintings, Room (Salon Dore) and Sculpture

"Sita and Sarita" (1921) was painted by Cecelia Beaux. It is an oil portrait of Sarah Leavitt. A portrait is an image of a specific person, and in this painting there is also a cat. Cecelia Beaux painted when there were few women artists. She was very successful. Do you have a pet? If you do, how would you pose your pet in a picture--what would your pet be doing?

"Salon Doré" is in the French language and means "Golden Room." It was built in 1770 and was part of a town house in Paris, France. Senator William Andrews Clark bought it, and it became part of his New York City mansion. It was donated to the Corcoran Gallery of Art after he died in 1925. It is the room that Midnight and Sita raced through and where they jumped over the clock that belonged to a queen. Do you live in a town house? Does it look like this? How is it different?

"Mt. Corcoran" (1875-77) was painted by Albert Bierstadt. This oil painting is a landscape painting--a painting of the land. It shows a mountain in the northwestern United States. The artist named the painting "Mt. Corcoran," and Mr. Corcoran purchased it for his gallery. What is in the distance (background) in the painting, and what is in the front (foreground)? How about the middle? There are different kinds of paint, like oil, acrylic and watercolor. Painting is lots of fun!

"The Mountain Man" (1903) was sculpted by Frederick Remington. This bronze sculpture depicts a cowboy on a horse descending a steep mountain. Remington loved the Wild West at a time when it was disappearing. He sculpted many cowboys and Native Americans. A sculpture has three dimensions (3D)--it is high, wide and deep. It can be made of different materials such as bronze, clay, marble and even plastic. If you have been horseback riding, did you have fun, and how did you feel afterwards?

"Niagara Falls" (1857) was painted by Frederick Edwin Church. This oil painting was a huge success and was called "Niagara without the roar." Niagara Falls was considered one of the wonders of the new world. Do you know where it is? Have you ever seen waterfalls?

As far as we know, the Corcoran Gallery of Art has no mice--but there might be a guard named Joe!

Made in the USA
Middletown, DE
10 December 2016